Ian Hamilton

The Ballad of Hádji, and Other Poems

Ian Hamilton

The Ballad of Hádji, and Other Poems

ISBN/EAN: 9783744711937

Printed in Europe, USA, Canada, Australia, Japan

Cover: Foto ©Andreas Hilbeck / pixelio.de

More available books at **www.hansebooks.com**

THE
BALLAD OF HÁDJI

AND OTHER POEMS

BY

IAN HAMILTON

LONDON

KEGAN PAUL, TRENCH, & CO.

MDCCCLXXXVII

CONTENTS.

CONTENTS.

THE BALLAD OF HÁDJI AND THE BOAR.

As I rode over the dusty waste
My dainty Arab's hoof-strokes traced
Glad rhythms in my mind,
Which seemed to murmur unto me
How he and I were lone and free
As wide Sahara's wind.

My heart beat high—the sun was bright—
And, as a beacon's startling light
Proclaims a threatening war,
My burnished lance-point met the glare
And flashed and sparkled in the air—
A pale and glancing star.

B

I saw a hawk pass hovering
Through the azure heights, on balanced wing ;
Its shadow fell down sheer
Upon my path, then onwards sped,
Smoother than gliding skaters tread
A fastly-frozen mere.

Thus heedless I, when suddenly
My Hádji broke the reverie
By stamping on the ground,
Whilst from a brake where grasses rank
Embraced the margin of a tank,
There came a rustling sound :

No long suspense ;—his bloodshot eyes
Aflame with sullen, fierce surprise—
Stepped out a grisly boar :
His gloomy aspect seemed to say—
" No other has the right to stray
Along this marsh-bound shore."

Now I had seen the life blood gush
From many a boar of nine-inch tush,
And so had Hádji too:
But never I ween had we either seen
So great a beast, so gaunt and lean,
So ugly to the view.

With others by to help at need,
Or give success applausive meed,
'Tis easy to be brave.
But when a man must do alone
Each danger seems more dismal grown;
Each petty ditch a grave.

And so—although the spear-point dropped—
As still as effigy I stopped,
Nor gave my steed the spur;
The more I looked, more gruesome grew
This king of all the swinish crew;
More prudence made demur.

But, as I hung in anguished doubt,
The marsh-born tyrant turned about,
As weary of the play;
He turned and dashed adown the glade
(No phantom now or goblin shade)
The well-known grisly gray:

And doubt no more distressed my mind;
In twenty years I'd never find
Such trophy to my lance,
For turning he had let me see
His tusks gigantic—shame 'twould be
If I had lost the chance.

I dropped my hand; when Hádji knew
The slackened rein away he flew
Across the belt of ooze;
The slim reeds rustled—till he sprang
Out on the plain whose surface rang
Beneath his iron shoes.

To left, to right, the wanton shied
At shadows, as in lusty pride
He rolled his dark fierce eye ;
Or gazing at our grim pursuit
He'd lay his ears back at the brute
And snort full savagely.

As minutes came, and lived, and went,
Ever the monster backward sent
The pebbles in my face,
Yet, when an hour was spent—at length
He seemed to fail in speed and strength
And nearer drew the chase.

But lo ! the impetuous Rávi ran
Before us; not a means to span
Its fiercely rushing stream ;
The boar sprang in—we never checked—
And followed ere the foam that flecked
His plunge had ceased to gleam.

Above our heads the yellow wave
Triumphant for an instant drave,
Then gaping gave us day;
It gave us day, and snorting loud
Bold Hádji stemmed the whirling crowd
Of surges topped with spray,

Aboard a skiff two children played,
No little whit were they dismayed
To see us swimming boldly;
One waved his hand in baby glee
When—overboard—most dismally
He slipped, to perish coldly.

The tender thing sank down below,
I marked its last convulsive throe,
But never paused to save.
I would—but just, I chanced to see
The boar bestrew the distant lea
With conquered Rávi's wave.

AND THE BOAR.

I turned me from the helpless thing,
I left it darkly struggling,
Nor hearkened to my soul ;
I swam beside my gallant steed ;
At length we touched the further reed,
And saved a ferry's toll.

But short as seemed the time we'd lost,
Long was the space of ground it cost.
Not to be covered soon ;
For distant dim the monster grim
Now flitted faint against the rim   .
Of the uprising moon.

Yes—like a bubble filled with smoke—
The curd-white moon upswimming broke
The vacancy of space,
Whilst sinking slowly at my back
The sun breathed blood-stains on the rack
Which veiled his dying face.

On, on, again ; the snow-fed flood
Had cooled the monster's heated blood,
And fresh and strong he fled :
An aged peasant crossed his path ;
He turned upon him in his wrath,
And left him there for dead.

The wretch implored me to remain
And staunch his wound—but all in vain—
I laughed to see his plight ;
For I was glad the boar had stayed
To wound the man, and so delayed
His headlong rapid flight.

And Hádji wearied not a whit,
For stretching free he'd take the bit
And hold it, or would fling
A foam-flake from his tossing head,
To glitter on his mane's silk thread,
Whilst ever galloping.

Ere long the arid landscape changed ;
A painter's eye had gladly ranged
Amidst its varied hue ;—
For far as mortal eye could reach,
As close as pebbles on the beach
Bright poppy flowers blew.

In countless gaudy chequered squares
Nepenthe grew for human cares—
Fair dreams for folk who weep,
And multitudes of drowsy bees
Forestalled the dreamy-eyed Chinese,
Sipping their honied sleep.

All else was silent ; not a bird
Disturbed the death of day or stirred
The calm air with a vesper,
But yet great Nature has her voice,
" Take peace or strife, thou hast the choice."
I heard the solemn whisper.

But should I draw my rein for this ?
Let dreamers prate of peaceful bliss—
Such fancies were diseased :
Large sweat-drops trickled from my brow,
The gaping furrows of the plough
Drank of us and were pleased.

The crimsons of the glowing west
In fainter ruddy shadows dressed
The mounting eastern moon ;
The slender-pillared palm-tree stems
Were sky-tinged too, as though from gems
Of garnet they were hewn.

And now when eve had lost its heat,
A Brahmin maiden stole to meet
Her sweetheart in the dusk ;
Her face adorned each lucid gem
Set round it :—to her garments' hem
Dripped essences of musk.

Her pensive mien and absent look,
Most plain betrayed a maid forsook
Of her own gentle heart ;
Outrunning time, she meets her lover,
About her lips dream-kisses hover,
They smile themselves apart.

The Fates know why—a cruel chance—
No lover's is the fatal glance
'Neath which the maiden cowers ;
No smiling gallant to her tripped,
But in an instant she lies ripped
And bleeding on the flowers.

" Sah'b ! Sah'b ! " she sobbed, " I bleed to death !
Ah, give your panting courser breath,
And call my lover here ! "
But rude and savage passions surged
Within my veins—*I madly urged
Poor Hádji with the spear.*

And he no longer fought the hand
Which forced his fleetness to command,
Or snorted to the breeze :
His breaths were choked with piteous sobs,
And I could feel his heart's wild throbs
Between my close-set knees.

His glossy coat no longer shone
Red golden as he galloped on,
And on ! without a check ;
Dank sweat had rusted it to black
Save where the reins had chafed a track,
Of snow along his neck.

The deepening twilight scarce revealed
Where flights of shadowy night-birds wheeled
And shrieking greeted us,
But never should my fixéd soul
Forsake the fast-approaching goal,
For omens timorous.

The jackals woke and like a rout
Of hell-loosed fiends, their eldritch shout
Was borne upon the breeze—
Ai! Ai! Ou! Ai!—a ghoulish scream,
And yet half-human ; like a dream
Of mortal agonies.

As I closed in on that evil beast
The champéd froth like creamy yeast
Bestreaked his grizzled hide ;
And like a small and smould'ring brand
His eye back-glancing ever scanned
Me creeping to his side.

Ha! Ha! He turned to charge and fight ;
I shouted out for pure delight,
And drove my spear-point in.
Clean through his body passed the steel—
I held him off—I made him reel—
Like chafer on a pin.

An instant so—then through the womb
Of night I galloped, and the gloom
Of jungles lone and drear ;—
But I had stricken, stricken home,
For on my hand his bloody foam
Had left a purple smear.

So circling back, I peered around,
And, by the moon, too soon I found
The grisly brute at bay :
His back was to a thorny tree,
I looked at him, and he at me ;—
There one of us would stay.

'Twas still as death—we charged together,
And in the dim and sightless weather
I struck him, but not true :
He seized the lance-shaft in his jaw
And split it as it were a straw,
Instead of good bamboo.

Then swift as thought the brute accursed,
Made fiercely in—at Hádji first—
Who much disdained to fly :
The little Arab shuddering stood—
Then fell—as monarchs of the wood
When cruel axes ply.

Ere I could rise, his tusk had cut
All down my back a gaping rut ;—
He gashed me deep and sore :
No weapon armed me for the strife,
But rage can fight without a knife,
I sprang upon the boar.

The thorn stretched out its sable claws,
And nodded with a black applause !
With fierce sepulchral glee
Three plantains whispered in a rank,
And clapped their fingers long and lank,
A ghostly gallery.

Above him now—then fallen beneath,
I tore him madly with my teeth,
Nor loosed my frantic hold ;
One finger searched the spear-head hole,
And dug there like a frightened mole
'Neath skin and fleshy fold :

I clung around his sinewy crest ;
He leaped, but could not yet divest
Himself of his alarm.
I hung as close as keepsake locket
On maiden breast—but, from its socket,
He wrenched my bridle-arm !

No more could I, and with a curse
I yielded to a last reverse,
And dropped upon the sand.
He glower'd o'er me—then drew back
To make more headlong the attack
Which nothing should withstand.

But, even then, he chanced to pass
The spot where dying lay—alas !—
Brave Hádji—desert-born ;
Not e'en that bristled front was proof
Against the Arab's arméd hoof—
His brains festooned the thorn.

Then I arose, all dripping red,
And gazed on him I oft had fed,
And wept to see him low :
No more he'd gallop in his pride—
No mortal man would e'er bestride
Poor Hádji here below.

He died amidst those jungles tangled ;
I staggered on all torn and mangled,
Gasping for painful breath ;
And when, beneath that placid moon,
My spirit left me in a swoon,
I'd known the worst of death.

Next day they found and bore me home,

And now, they say, I'll never roam

The glades and forests hoar ;

No more, they say, I'll ever wield

The spear in sport or battle-field,

Or ride the grisly boar.

TO FLOWERS.

Most exquisitely fair and fragile flowers,
Unearthly figures that our Earth doth use
To mark the flight of months of wingéd hours
With varying letters, writ in heavenly hues,
I love you ! I could ponder half a day
On the deep blush that mantles in a rose,
And picture fantasies and melt away
My heart, where clustering the lilac blows.
  Oft seated in a sombre, sighing glade
Dejected, I have watched the wanton breeze
Stir all the chequers of the light and shade
Till the dark grass grew restless as the seas:
Then—like those kindest kisses that are given
Apart from crowds and gaily-peopled streets—
Some lurking violet has shyly striven
To breathe how even gloomiest woods held sweets.

Anon refreshed, I wander o'er a wold
Whose glimmering green velvets are enriched
With daisy broideries of white and gold ;
By fairy needles surely they were stitched
In such a starred confusion ; cowslips slender
Lend here their bosoms to bright butterflies
Who, flutter indecisive, ere they render
To kindred blooms the pollen's soft, sweet dyes :

Or by some willow, where the glassy wave
Scarce steals away, so sluggish is the stream,
A water-lily leaves the sunless grave
Which shrouds its root, and floats there like a
　　　dream
Dreamt by a mortal, cleaving limpid space,
Whilst far beneath, all steeped in leaden sleep,
His body lies, nor ever can retrace
What its soul witnessed in that slumber deep.

Oh flowers, when I gaze on you and drink
Your liquid perfumes thrilling in the wind,
You have a power lent you to unlink
Those clasps of clay which keep my spirit blind :

Then, sometimes then—surpassing Death and
    Sin—
My soul, half-conscious, glances out afar
Through the close web our finite senses spin
To veil from us who, what, or whence we are.

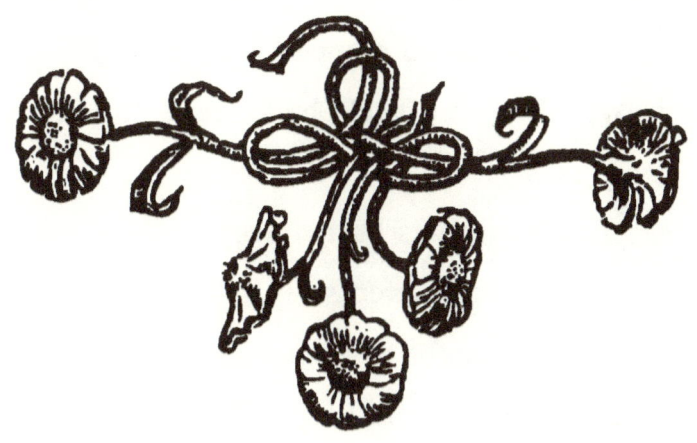

CHILD-LIFE.

'Tis gone !—and so long past
That wisdom should forget it ;—yet again
One backward glance I'll cast
And joys fallen sere shall build dead childhood's
       fane :
    For Youth lies buried deep—
    Lost in enchanted sleep—
Sunk in the depths of Memory's cold lake
Whose crystal waters keep old days awake
In semblance only, for no man may slake
His pleasure on the Past.

    Yes, Youth is dead and gone—
Youth when the future loomed not pale and wan,
    But when I deemed that any hour
    Might haply bring the blissful dower

Anticipated ever ;—till at length,
With dimming eyes and failing strength,
Rude disillusion bade me learn
That men may never, never earn
Whilst dwelling here, contentment holy,
But, destined prey to melancholy,
Their visions transplanted be
From time into Eternity.

In my glad childhood nought of this
Perturbed my Paradise of bliss ;
In summer days each lingering second
Counted an hour as grown folk reckoned ;
And, stretching vast, my afternoon
Contained at least an old man's June :
One butterfly was fortune more
Than tons on tons of richest ore,
And my white rabbit, pinky-eyed,
Gave me the charms of empire wide.

'Twas winter ! Lo, the window panes
Were arabesqued with frosty stains,

And—glorious prospect—from a cloud
Fell floating fast Earth's chill white shroud.
Then Christmas, and the mystic tree
All stuck with tapers daintily ;
Red and blue and green, they showed
Branches bending to their load
Of tinsel gear, a costly hoard,
My envied share a wooden sword.
At night, attired in velvet frock,
Both soft and rich, I'd wait the knock
Which called me to untimely bed :
Till then, full eagerly I read
Good books, and nestling by the fire
Which sparkled gay, I'd much admire
How true men throve, and villains fell,
And vow this earth was ordered well.
Winter, summer, night and day,
Lesson hours, and hours of play,
Still I imagined life was fine
And wished the age of twenty mine,
When I might play a leading part

And win some lovely lady's heart
Losing mine own ; for even then
I'd heard of love, and envied men.

Now older grown, I'd build brave stories
Within my mind, of martial glories ;
Through desperate fights a coal-black steed
Bore me unharmed with magic speed,
And then as Harold I would pose,
Or with fierce Murat charge my foes :
Till, changed the spirit of my dream
And o'er the soft seas' restless gleam
My comrades and myself would rove,
Sharing plump sacks of treasure-trove :
Or cruising down the lazy "trades"
Where the dim horizon fades
On coral islands plumed with palms,
Whose folk die old, nor know the qualms
Of restless longing.

Like crystals soon old love-thoughts grew,
And from the vague child-wonder drew

Colours to paint an angel form
With shape and fair consistence warm.
The purest mind that ever breathed
About my brow the laurel wreathed ;
I loved her—mishaps followed fast—
But fate grew kinder, till, at last,
I've dreamed we wed.

Thus did my glance
Travel the wavering mists of chance,
Whilst endless vistas of delight
Beckoned me on with prospects bright.

But false was all the air-drawn splendour
Which fancy to young hope did render :
As Dead Sea apples to the taste,
As mirage o'er a thirsty waste,
Sink youthful hopes of splendid hue
When manhood grasps them as its due.

Man of wisdom ;—cull the pleasant

From an ever-dying present,

" Joys as wingéd dreams fly fast "—

All is passing—nought may last !

TO CLOUDS.

I.

Fair evanescent forms that spring from earth
Whene'er the sun does amorously burn,
And soft-limbed sea bears a yet softer birth
To his hot kisses.   Proudly do you spurn
Our boundaries, and heaven-expiring yearn
To crack your chains !   Not yet have you escaped :
Dissolved in tears Fate dooms you to return,
Foiled like those schemes Philosophy has shaped.

II.

As lordly icebergs float upon the main,
You drift along the azure ebb and flow
Of airy currents, innocent of stain,
Pale as the presence of your daughter snow,
Your grateful shadows fall on us below.
Oft then sky-pavéd battlements unfold
Pure as smooth-carven marble, till the glow
Of dying day steeps all their towers in gold.

III.

Or should you chance to frame a gloomy form
Whose huge limbs tramp athwart the wintry sky,
Behold ! an onslaught of the assaulting storm
Makes yet more weird the figure we descry—
Then rends it—whilst each gust that hurtles by
Seems to bear with it on its mighty wing
A whispered, awful, agonizing sigh
Wrung from the wreck of that gigantic thing.

IV.

But when you close upon us, oh ! chill clouds,
As dull and grey as any coffin's lead,
And drape Heaven's portals in your envious shrouds
Till bright stars fade and very space has fled ;
We long to clip your sea-fledged pinion-spread,
Rejoicing much when your own dismal womb
Breeds the wild infant that must strike you dead—
And cloud-born bolts disperse their natal gloom.

REGRET.

I dreamed a dream on that night of nights—
    Bright shone the morning star,
As an angel cleft the diamond heights
    Bearing my fancies far,

And he flapped his vast and shadowy pinion
    Against the ebon air,
Until we reached the fair dominion
    Which Youth and Spring-time share :

Lost amidst whispering forest dells,
    I lay—well awake—no dreamer ;
A moonbeam fondled the young blue-bells
    And danced with the jessamine streamer :

All down the mystic glimmering glade
    Pale roses tremblingly

Greeted the faint airs which conveyed
   Their fragrances to me :

Large butterflies were trooping by
   With golden wings of splendour—
Upon my ear a sad sweet sigh
   Expired in accents tender :

Ah—how came she there—and whence came she ?
   For I lay 'midst the flowers at her feet—
And I sighed, and she stooped to kiss me—
   But,— I woke ere our mouths could meet !

STILL IS THE SPOT.

Still is the spot where Merlin slumbers well—
But not more still than this my favourite dell ;
Its three huge beeches rear themselves aloft,
And half-concealed by bracken lull and soft
A dark pool glimmers.
Of humble height, yet lovely in their hue,
The courtier wild flowers pay obeisance due
To each great gnarléd root.   The green arcades
Of foliage fling a shadow on the glades
Which gently shimmers.
And hark ! a goldfinch piping to his mate.
The cup runs over ; neither care nor hate
Nor grisly fear itself, can break the spell
Which Nature sets about my woodland dell.
Life is sufficient—rash it were to look
One single step beyond this fairy nook.

But—comes a day, when winter's iron hand
Has struck the spot where my three beeches stand :
The flowers lie dead—the leaves are rent away,
And all the land looks desolate and grey.
The tolling of a distant solemn bell
Invades my ruined refuge ; few can tell
I trust, the hopeless sorrows that may spring
To such a sound from transient slumbering.

So there I stand, and miserably grieve
My lot—till looking upwards I perceive
How much more clear the ethereal heavens are
    seen
When the stark boughs lament their robes of
    green !
Those fading forms which were the summer's pride,
And my delight, had flourished but to hide
God's heaven where Hope slept 'neath a canopy
Unwrought with stars—slept, but eternity
Dwells there and Hope awakes.

So, too, when Death has robbed us of a friend
We first feel sure this world is not an end ;
For high Philosophy most oft imparts
Her golden gift to sad and chastened hearts.

LOST LOVE.

1.

Lost Love, when Summer stands above my head·—
His azure banner swept across the sky—
And sets the evenings in a glow of red,
And paints his morn with tender greenish dye;
When Nature lives as though Death's self were dead;
Then—though the universe be wholly glad—
Since thou hast passed away, such joy but makes
     me sad.

2.

When thrilling 'neath the faint warm July breeze
The tender shoots break into coloured fire
And sick with love implore the yellow bees
To play the pander to their hot desire;
When thrushes make glad warble 'midst the trees,
Interpreting love's languors in their choir,
I sigh no more to see life speeding by;
What only brings regret can scarce too swiftly fly.

3.

When thou wast by, the black and biting frost

Seemed sent to lullaby the restless lake,

And icéd storms grew playful when they tost

Huge coiling billows in the stout ships wake ;

E'en cruel snows had all their treachery lost,

And wandered down with every feathered flake

A splendid jewel—glancing to and fro

But that mine own lost love was long six months
    ago.

4.

Ah then, exalted that my love was near,

I viewed this world exceedingly content :

To boundless admiration sea and sphere

Bore wave or star harmoniously blent

And love ruled all that now lies dull and sere

Without one sign of heavenly intent

Graven upon it :—since thy death, oh love !

Dark grows the orbéd world and dim the stars
    above.

THE DEATH-THROES OF MR. WORLDLY
REASON.

Girl of the soft blue eyes
   You I am wooing ;—
Where are my maxims wise—
   What am I doing?

Tell me your pedigree,
   Answer me, Madam !
Can your vague family tree
   Say more than " Adam "?

No ; well then please explain
   Why I am wooing ;
Where is the good or gain
   I am pursuing?

Maybe you've learning and
  Love " logs " and statics—
What ! you don't understand
  " Much Mathematics " !

Have you then mastered Greek ?
  Can you quote Latin ?
I fear you'd rather speak
  Silken and satin.

Lass with the tender smile—
  Are you an heiress ?
Have you a golden pile
  Worthy a Mayoress ?

Or does your only gold
  Gleam from those tresses ?
Whilst I both weak and bold
  Pay you addresses.

Give me your hand, my dear—
   Best friends must sever—
This is goodbye, I fear,
   Goodbye for ever !

But even as we part,   .
   Hand in hand lingers ;
Closely about my heart
   Wind your slim fingers.

Something is all amiss—
   My pulses flutter—
I speak the word it is
   Madness to utter !

     *   *   *

A HONEYMOON SONG.

The moon turns piteous pale—the rose burns soft
In her emerald bowers !   Eastwards the pavilion
Of dawn is blazoned with a faint vermilion :
The violet lifts her dewy eye aloft,
And to the impulse of the breath of morn
All the slim rushes by the silver mere
Dance, as the air-stirred lilacs shed a tear
Of incense on the dark and verdurous lawn.

Awake, my sweet ! open those orbs of lustre
Now dimmed deliciously by night's caresses ;
Open thy deep eyes !—what soft dream impresses
Its languors on thy soul !   Shake back that cluster
Which shades each lid with gold !   O come and
         wander
To banks where buds grown bashful in their hues
Peep shyly out ; there wearied love renews
That   passion   hoard   we   spendthrifts   live   to
         squander.

APRIL IN INDIA.

This is a month when in the West
    The milder air no more denies
A leafy screen to birds that nest ;
    When country strollers may surprise
    Shy violets masked in green disguise ;
When languors faint pervade the wind
    Foreshadowing Summer's perfumed sighs !
When th' elements have all combined
To bid each earth-born thing to be of cheerful mind.

But here,—such joyance as we had
    Has fled the fatal arid plain,
And exile presses doubly sad
    Till June arrives with freshening rain ;
    For smiles are very hard to feign
When April's sun begins to glare
    And dart fierce rays with might and main :
Then mournfully do mortals fare
Who gasp with sick distaste the oven-heated air.

See ! Fortune's favourites wildly fly
　　This torrid month and climb the hills ;
But I shall never scale the sky,
　　No hope of such illusion fills
　　My dream with plash of mountain rills :
Children and wife ?—Yes,—they may go,
　　And 'scape the furnace blast that kills,
But I must labour on below
And suffer, worst of all, sad separation's throe.

Still,—futile plaints are worse than nought,—
　　And so I do my duty here,
Sustained in India by the thought
　　Of days to come when Phœbus' fear
　　No more shall cause departure's tear ;
When, wife and children by my side,
　　May safely bide the livelong year,
And then no longer will I chide
Sweet Summer's harbinger, young April daisy-pied.

TO OUR OWN BEECH TREE.

When last I sat in shade of thee—
King of the forest—beechen tree,
A foliaged crown stood on thy head
Whose leaves, like brilliants, flaméd red
And gold—for soon they would be dead,
O ! misery.

When last I sat in shade of thee,
The sweetest maiden sat by me ;
Now maid and crown of gold have flown—
Forest and frozen wind make moan—
And thou and I stand here alone—
In misery.

DAYBREAK IN THE JUNGLE.

Lost in the jungle's tangle
I've watched the stars bespangle
  The dim blue firmament,
Till Dawn spread upwards, stealing
Their radiance, and revealing
  The flower founts of scent ;

Waking the clear fresh morning,
With jewel tints adorning
  Pale dew-drops of the night :
A soft, sweet wind passed sighing
And set the wet leaves crying
  That stars were put to flight.

Then rose the King of Splendour ;
With kisses golden, tender,
  Their fluttering hearts were woo'd ;
Soon to his beams beguiling
Those fickle leaves were smiling
  And changed their tearful mood.

LINES

WRITTEN IN THE TRAVELLER'S BUNGALOW

WHICH OVERHANGS THE FALLS

OF GERSAPPA.

I.

Smoothly sweeping, softly gleaming,

   Onwards to her lord the sea ;

Smiling to herself and dreaming

   Of her Ocean destiny ;

Rolls along this Indian river

Calm—without a prescient shiver—

Save when dark rocks, through her bubbles

Reflect a gloom, like hidden troubles.

2.

Sudden, flies her fond illusion !

   Hideous—sheer— a chasm grins

And in tossing mad confusion
Shuddering, her fall begins :
Lo, like molten Venice glasses
Rainbow-hued, Gersappa passes ;
How her masses leap and clamber
White or yellow, pearl and amber !

3.

Far below—like snow-flakes driven
By the blast ;—then smoky rings
Floating, till the waters riven
Turn to vapour as she sings,
"Fiercely still this rock-fanged chasm
Pales my depths with tortured spasm—
Shall I never wed with Ocean,
Never more have rest from motion ? "

4.

As she moans this piteous ditty
(Hearken, reader, to her prayer),

On her pangs the gods take pity,
  Let her bind her storm-tossed hair ;
Purity, the fall has taught her ;
Winds have cleansed her turgid water ;
Clear as crystal see her wending
Worthy of a bridal ending.

LINES ON LEAVING GERSAPPA.

I'd gladly live a forest life
    And wear the Lincoln green ;
No carking care or social strife
    Could touch me here, I ween.

The jungle-cock should waken me,
    To chase the sámbur stag,
Or else, to fell some mighty tree
    That clothes Gersappa's crag.

Oft dreaming in the woodland hoar
    I'd smoke my mild cheroot ;
And hearken to the torrents' roar
    And watch its waters shoot.

I'd muse upon the aims of men
    Pursuing shadows vain ;
I'd wander down a blossoming glen
    And soon I'd smile again.

Alas ! I hear my fortunes cry,
  " Far hence—lies your career ! "
And yet, e'en though I struggle high
  My happiness lay here.

Farewell, green forest, we must part ;
  Farewell, ye waving trees !
But graven on my inmost heart
  I bear your memories.

THEME.

I AM WEARY OF MINUTE ISOLATION.

O, Thou who art the universal source
From whose deep roots my mortal being flowers—
Take me again as skies reclasp their showers;
    Take my lost soul, and end this life's divorce !

Caught to thy bosom, once more I should be
A part of Thee—oh, formless, awful Life,
Severed from whom we suffer storm and strife,
    Penned into time from our eternity.

A woman seemed to make my life less weary
[She who perhaps formed part of me awhile—
Long ages since—came here to make me smile].
    But she is dead, and I am lone and dreary.
    O, take me back ! dissolve me, waft me, end me !
And make this small identity a blur,
A part of thee to be one thing with her :—
    Into thyself beneficently blend me !

DESPAIR.

Stars upon stars upon stars for ever !
Limitless regions !—Christ deliver
My soul from the terrors of infinite distance ;
My flesh from the curse of an endless existence.

.

God of my fathers, where art thou—Hearken !
Unto my prayer—for the waters darken
Over our heads and no sign is given,
Though worms make war upon highest Heaven.

ONE NIGHT MY SPIRIT.

One night my spirit wandered far
  Unfettered by gross human senses,
And saw earth shrivel to a star,
  And witnessed where the all commences.

A swift stream flowed ; some called it Chance,
  And some the force of Law unfailing,
O'er whose intricate waved expanse
  The lives of men passed sailing, sailing.

Minute unnumbered bubble-forms
  Spun giddily down that troubled river,
And on they sped—like storm-tossed wrecks,
  Whose fleets would vanish thence for ever :

And yet, methought each one that broke
  And melted to its river mother,

New lives to larger living woke,
  And Death and Life were one the other.

For far-feared death, it seemed to me,
  Was friend to progress—was renewal,
And without this no life could be ;
  Life was the flame, dark Death its fuel.

Each life that faded, so I dreamed,
  Was life at profit well expended ;
As Curtius leapt and Rome redeemed,
  So nobler life on death depended.

SONNET.

Lost in a dream, I watched a spreading palm,
   Until the full-orbed and majestic moon
   Broke from its plumes and lent the black lagoon
A golden bridge to span its waters calm.
And drifting there I marked a little craft
   Yield to some tide it could not well resist ;
   Boldly it left the vague and wavering mist
To cross this track on which gold ripplets laughed.

Swimming in light, it glittered gay and shone
   With tender, dainty hues, until it wore
A more than mortal sheen ; then, passing on,
   Grew duller far that it had gleamed before.
Thus, for a space, I flushed beneath your ray
   And then, alas ! swept on forlorn and gray.

A RUNAWAY SONNET.

There is an island bedded like a gem
 On the deep bosom of a tranquil sea :
 Love, I entreat thee, come !—though all condemn
My lost career and opportunity
Unrivalled yet renounced ;—for what is fame,
 Or others' voices to thine azure eyes ?
 See, I have set ambition in the frame
Of thy long lashes—there's the single prize

I care to strive for :—let a blind world cherish
 Its hollow pomps—I only would explore
The temple of Love's universe—then perish—
 For loveless life is death and something more ;
Answer me, love ! The wretched minutes
  languish
 As silence slowly crowns suspense with anguish.

TO ENDYMION AND ALL DAY-
DREAMS.

Ere the pale moon with chaste and icy light
    Had threaded silver through the birchen spray,
    Endymion would hie him far away
From populous haunts—a melancholy wight.
But when the cold rays of the Queen of Night
    Slid o'er his features ;—thus the poets say ;—
    Diana's self no more through Heaven might stray,
But left for him the vaulted azure height.

World despised dreamer, thou wast fortunate,
    Fixing thy hopes on an immortal bride :—
Secure possession might not satiate
    Thy first fresh love with its lethargic tide,
Nor custom and fatigue combine to abate
    Young passion's edge by whispering "fancy lied."

SONNET

You order me to take my pen and write
   In praise of Her—" the only girl "—ah me !
   I *can't* select a special only SHE
From all of those whose sweetness I'd requite :
Your limitation cramps poetic flight ;
   My wings are clogged, my Muse is all at sea ;
   I'd gladly sing of five or even three,
But one's invidious ; 'twould not be polite !

Two hundred loves have caused my heart to burn,
   Two hundred more, so help me ! Ill pursue :
To all your sex I'll lavish out in turn
   My pent-up passion—is it not their due !
Till, when my thirties never can return,
   I'll search the world for One resembling You.

LINES TO LADY —— ON HER
BIRTHDAY.

This morn, Miladi, sees you forty-five ;
You told us so ; 'tis not in you to strive
To force back Time's inevitable pace
With quibbles, as though age bespoke disgrace.
　Does your heart ache, another year has flown ?
No—surely no !—for not on you alone
Does Chronos frown :—we, all of us together,
Press onward towards the end, through every
　　weather ;
And lonesome you would feel, if anchored fast
'Midst life's swift stream, you saw us hurrying past.
　Though short our span, and though the thought-
　　less weep
And moan, that they shall never live to reap

What they had sown ; yet, deeds shall mock the
      bier,
For no man's work from earth may disappear—
Thus then it comes, Miladi, that I pray
You may enjoy your hundredth natal day.

AMBITION'S AVOWAL.

At life's fresh dawning,
Where the roads sever,
I pressed on scorning
All but endeavour.
Love seemed sheer folly
I was so clever,
Now Melancholy
Claims me for ever
Youth returns never!

TO EDITH.

To fix some thought that should awhile endure
Upon life's sand, I wearily have tried,
But, as I trace the characters,—full sure,
All is effaced by Time's remorseless tide.
Less lasting I, than bubbles filled with air,
Or fleeting shadows fallen from a cloud.
The sword above me trembles by a hair,
Oblivion hastes to lap me in her shroud.
Yet stay—my Fortune is not all unkind ;
See !   In an angel's aspect She appears
And proffers immortality combined
With present pleasure—cease then idle tears !
   For I may write a verse in Edith's praise,
   With such a theme 'twill live unnumbered days.

TO MISS SHERSTON ON HER
BIRTHDAY.

Upon the pleasant first of May
Was Mabel born ; then swift, I say,
Bring liquor ! I've a proper thirst on—
Here's happiness to Mabel Sherston !
More evanescent be her troubles
Than these sparkling purple bubbles
Which dance an instant in the cup
Ere—pouf !—I hold it bottom up !

THE FORCE OF CIRCUMSTANCE.

Ah, were I the Prince, and she Cinderella,

How swiftly—how frankly—I'd woo her and tell
    her

The thought which lies deep in my breast ;—

But alas cruel Fortune her malice evinces,

I still remain I,—and my sweetheart's a Princess ;

So with pain all the love is repressed !

I. H. TO N. C.

ON HIS DETERMINATION TO GET UP AT 6 A.M.

INSTEAD OF 7 A.M.

To save my youth from sere decay
    And gain more leisure for my rhyme
I've snatched one precious hour a day
To spend before my hair is grey.

I'm lingering on life's lightning way,
    And from relentless Father Time
I've snatched one precious hour a day
To spend before my hair is grey.

N. C. TO I. H.

ON HIS DETERMINATION TO GET UP AT 9.30

A.M. INSTEAD OF 8.30 A.M.

Lulled by the foolish crowing cocks,
And careless of the anxious clocks,
I lie—nor don my chilly socks—
     One hour a day.

Far from the conflicts of the world
Within my little bed I'm curled ;
Hark ! 'tis my nose expels the air
With more than trumpet-like fanfare.
Thus from those cares that make men grey
     I gain at least *one* hour a day.

F

SUNRISE.

The lusty Sun,
Rolling his jolly face above those hills
Which frame vast space with saffron window-sills,
Kisses pale Earth with flame-moustacheoed lip :
　She, blushing crimson, hastily does strip
Her sleeping weed of black and barren gloom
The freer to absorb his fervid ray ;
Until, in fond return, her teeming womb
Bears purple grapes, gold corn and olives grey.

A SONG OF COMMON SENSE IN LOVE.

Afar my thoughts are borne—
They speed to where this heart forlorn
First learnt to throb for thee ;
Where first a spark escaped thine eyes
To kindle into burning sighs
Love sleeping dreamlessly.

Are those eyes cold—once fond and frank—
Is thy glance faded, chill and blank—
To pangs it fostered—dead ?
Say, was it like the fuse's flash
Which fires a mine, then sinks in ash
Whilst flame and ruin spread ?

The sad pale moon views my despair
What time warm sunbeams kiss thine hair,

So wide apart are we :
Between us mighty Oceans flow
And many a vagrant breeze does blow—
Ah, thinkest thou of me ?

No word or sign !   Is't even so ?
For nought I waste my nights in woe—
For nought I've writ of thee ?
Then fare-thee-well, forgetful maid,
Thy worth seems slight when coolly weighed ;
I'm gladly quit of thee !

AN APPEAL.

When the black vessel loses land ;
When distance dims the sun-gilt strand ;
When faint the waving palm trees stand—
                    One sigh for me !

When brine-bedewed these roses die
And withered and neglected lie,
Reck of my withering heart and try
                    To think of me.

.The magnet needle holds its goal
Still faithful to the frozen pole ;
Be not thus frigid to the soul
                    Which clings to thee.

If lonely, severed from his mate,

Some storm-chased bird should calm await

On your tall mast ; I share its fate,

        So pity me.

Oft towards some radiant star you'll steer

[A starless night is full of fear]

You were my star—Oh, beacon clear,

        Shine on for me !

ALAS!

Dreaming I float my soul away,
    Whilst my seeming self sits laughing loud :--
    At trifling jests which please the crowd
I laugh, but I think of a bye-gone day.
I think of when first I saw you—
    Softly gleamed your golden-threaded hair ;
    Its lustre first kindled this fierce despair,
Then first to tranquil days I bade adieu.

Dreaming sad dreams of might have been,
    Round me gaily rings the jest,
    With seeming zest I laugh my best—
But I sigh the more in my thoughts unseen.
Again, once again, I meet you ;
    Ah, the price such Memories may cost !
    A summer so short, then unending frost ;
The lightning's golden flash, then midnight's hue.

Eating my heart in hot unrest

    Whilst my outward mask disdains

    To show its pains, and ne'er complains,

But laughs the louder for its canker guest—

I think of when last I saw you—

    Cruel ocean snatched you from my sight ;

    With dreadful hastening speed, my star, my

        light !

The fatal ship speeds on—Alas—Adieu !

www.ingramcontent.com/pod-product-compliance
Lightning Source LLC
Chambersburg PA
CBHW030011030726
47499CB00008B/2993